W9-BJU-181

Juvenile Historical
Collection

A GIFT OF
Martha Bennett King

The Denver Public Library

SALT

SALT

A Russian tale adapted by Harve Zemach

from a literal translation, by Benjamin Zemach,
of the Russian of Alexei Afanasev

with Illustrations by
MARGOT ZEMACH

Follett Publishing Company

Chicago

Library of Congress Catalog Card Number: 65-12312

Copyright © 1965, by Margot Zemach. All rights reserved.
No part of this book may be reproduced in any form
without written permission from the publisher. Manufactured
in the United States of America. Published simultaneously
in Canada by The Ryerson Press, Toronto.

123456789

SALT

LONG AGO there lived a merchant who had three sons. The first was Fyodor, the second Vasily, and the third Ivan—Ivan the Fool.

This merchant was rich. He sent his ships over the ocean in all directions to trade goods in foreign lands. Once he loaded two ships with precious furs, wax, and honey, and sent them sailing with his two elder sons. But when Ivan asked for the same, the merchant refused, saying: "You would do nothing but sing songs to the moon, and try to make the fishes dance, and come home without your head."

However, when he saw how much his son wanted to go, he gave him a ship with the very cheapest cargo of beams and boards.

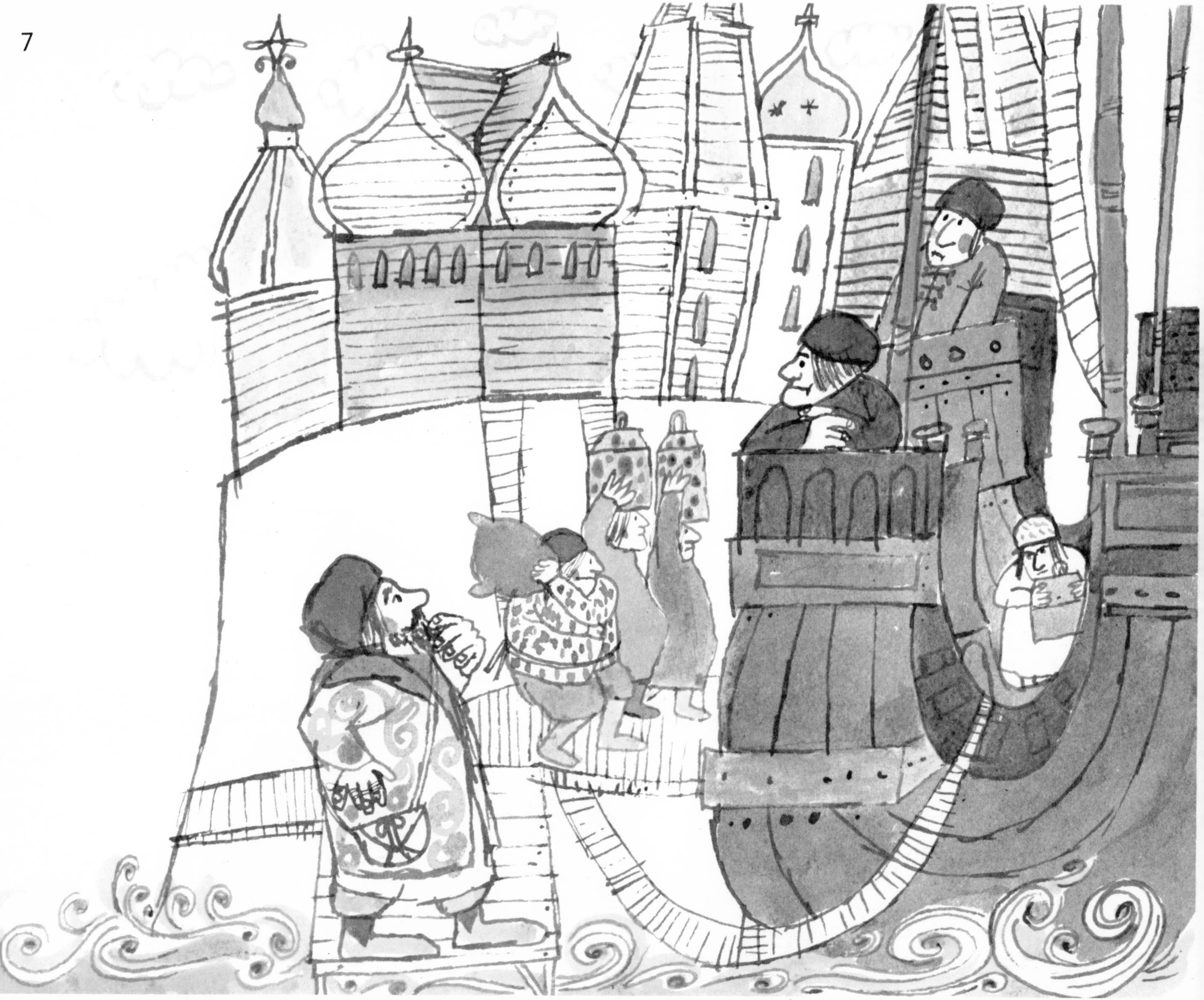

Ivan prepared for the journey, set sail, and soon caught up with his brothers. They sailed together for a day or two, until a strong wind came up and blew away Ivan's ship into uncharted seas.

The wind blew Ivan and his crew to the north and to the south. At last they reached an island. Ivan stepped out upon the shore and found a path which led to the top of a mountain. There he discovered that this mountain was not made of rock, nor of sand, nor of stone, but of salt—pure Russian salt.

Without delay he ordered his sailors to throw away all the boards and beams, and to load the ship with salt. As soon as this was done, Ivan set forth once more.

After a long time or a short time, either nearby or far away, the ship arrived at a large city. Ivan went into the city to bow before the king and request permission to trade his merchandise. He took a bundle of the salt with him. The king greeted him in a friendly manner and heard his request.

"And what kind of goods do you sell?" asked the king.

"Russian salt, Your Majesty," said Ivan, showing him the contents of his bundle.

The king had never heard of salt. The people of his kingdom ate all their food without salt. When he saw what Ivan showed him, he thought it was only white sand.

"Well, little brother," he said to Ivan, "we have all we need of this. No one will pay you money for it."

Ivan turned away feeling very disappointed. Then he thought to himself: "Why don't I go to the king's kitchen and see how the cooks prepare the food and what kind of salt they use." He went and watched the cooks running back and forth, boiling and roasting and pouring and mixing. But no one put a single grain of salt in the food.

Ivan waited his chance and then secretly poured the right amount of salt into all the stews and sauces.

When the first dish was served to the king, he ate of it and found it more tasty than ever before. The second dish was served, and he liked it even better.

Then the king called for his cooks and said to them: "In all the years that I have been king, you have never cooked me such a delicious meal. How did you do it?"

The cooks answered: "Your Majesty, we cooked the same as ever. But the merchant who asked your permission to trade was watching us. Perhaps he added something to the food."

"Send for him!" commanded the king.

Then Ivan, the merchant's son, was brought before the king. He fell on his knees and confessed his guilt.

"Forgive me, Your Majesty," he begged. "I put Russian salt in all the stews and sauces. That's the way we do it in my country."

"And what is the price of this salt?" asked the king.

Ivan realized his advantage and said: "Not very much—for two measures of salt, give me one measure of silver and one of gold."

The king agreed to this price and bought the entire cargo. Ivan filled his ship with silver and gold and made ready to sail for home.

Now the king had a daughter, a beautiful princess. Attended by her maid-servants, she went down to the port to see the Russian ship. Ivan the Fool just then was strumming a tune. The melody reached the ears of the princess, and its sweetness entered her heart.

It was not long before Ivan and the beautiful princess stood together before the king to receive his blessing. To the sound of trumpets and the cheers of the king's subjects, Ivan and the princess departed from the city and sailed forth on a favorable wind.

For a long time, for a short time, Ivan and the princess sailed the sea. Then his elder brothers appeared across his path. They learned of his good luck and were very jealous.

They boarded his ship, seized him, and threw him into the sea. Then they divided the booty; Fyodor, the eldest brother, took the princess, and Vasily, the second brother, took the ship full of silver and gold.

Now it happened that when they flung Ivan from the ship, one of the boards that he himself had thrown into the sea was floating nearby. He grabbed hold of this board and for a long time was tossed upon the waves. Finally he was carried to an unknown island. No sooner had he landed on the shore, when along came a gloomy giant with an enormous mustache, from which hung a huge pair of mittens, drying after the rain.

"What do you want here?" asked the giant. Ivan told him everything that had happened.

The gloomy giant sighed and said: "Come along, I will carry you home. Tomorrow your eldest brother is to marry the princess. Sit on my back."

The giant lifted Ivan, set him on his back, and raced across the sea. Soon Ivan could see his native land ahead, and moments later they arrived. The giant put him down, saying: "Now promise not to boast to anyone about riding on my back. Don't try to make fun of me. If you do, I shall grab you up and toss you back into the sea."

Ivan, the merchant's son, promised not to boast, thanked the giant, and went home.

He arrived just as the wedding procession was about to enter the church. When the princess saw him, she cried aloud and tore herself away from Fyodor, the eldest brother.

"This is the one I must marry," she said, "and not the other."

"What's that?" asked the father.

Ivan told him everything—how he had traded the salt, how he had won the favor of the princess, and how his brothers had thrown him into the sea.

The father got very angry at his elder sons, called them scoundrels, and married Ivan to the princess.

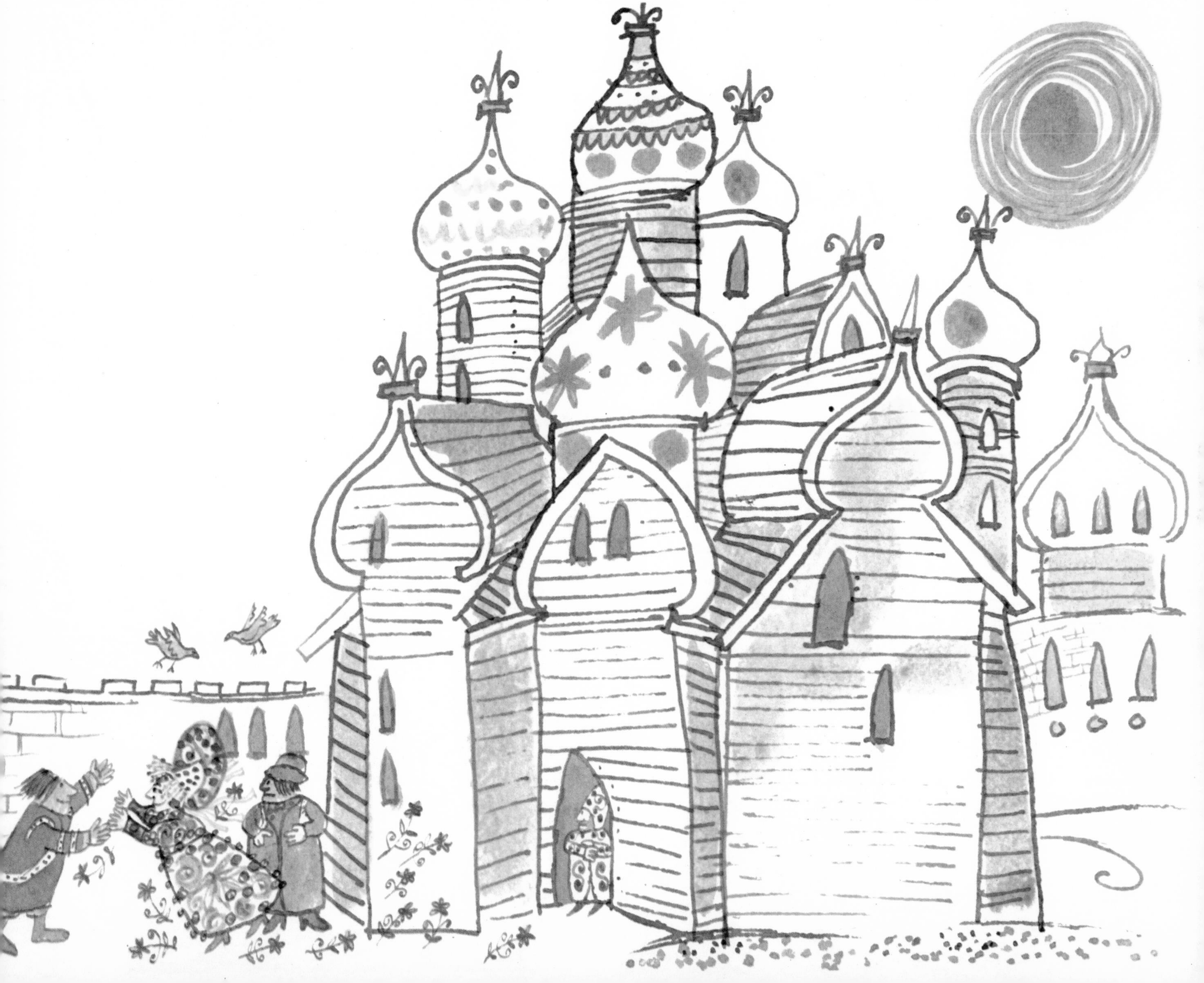

There now began a joyful feast. The guests ate and drank and made merry. The men began to boast, some about their strength, some about their riches, some about their beautiful wives. And Ivan the Fool happily boasted too: "Listen to this! I really have something to boast about! A giant carried me piggyback across the sea!"

As soon as he said these words, the giant appeared at the gate.

"Ah, Ivan!" said the gloomy giant. "You promised not to boast about me. Now what have you done?"

"Forgive me!" cried Ivan. "It was not really I that boasted, but my happiness."

"Come, show me what you mean," said the giant. "What do you mean by happiness?"

Then Ivan took up his mandolin, and played and danced the best he knew how. And his playing and dancing was so filled with happiness that all the guests danced and clapped their hands. And soon the gloomy giant let himself smile and kept time to the music with his feet.

"Well, Ivan," he said at last, "now I know what happiness is. You may boast about me all you like."

So the wedding feast continued, and the giant departed, and Ivan the Fool and the beautiful princess lived happily ever after.